Who Owns the Cow?

by Andrew Clements · Illustrated by Joan Landis

Clarion Books/New York

Clarion Books ✶ a Houghton Mifflin Company imprint ✶ 215 Park Avenue South, New York, NY 10003
Text copyright © 1995 by Andrew Clements ✶ Illustrations copyright © 1995 by Joan Landis
The illustrations for this book were executed in acrylics. ✶ The text was set in 18/24-point Americana.

Library of Congress Cataloging-in-Publication Data

Clements, Andrew, 1949–   Who owns the cow? / by Andrew Clements ; illustrated by Joan Landis. ✶ p.   cm.
Summary: In a sense, the farmer's cow is also owned by the neighbor girl who thinks about her, the milkman who buys her milk,
the painter who paints her, and any others who appreciate her. ✶ ISBN 0-395-70145-7 ✶ [1. Cows—Fiction.]   I. Landis, Joan, ill.
II. Title.   PZ7.C59118Wh   1996   [E]—dc20   94-19308   CIP   AC
TWP 10 9 8 7 6 5 4 3 2 1

1 COW

4

The farmer bought the cow,
and the farmer bought the field,
and the field grows the grass,
and the grass feeds the cow,
so the farmer owns the cow.

There's a bell around the neck
of the cow that's in the field,
and when the cow is milked each morning,
she walks up to the barn.
When she walks the bell goes clanking,
and its clanking fills the air,

and the air goes through the window
of the house just up the road.
The girl inside the house lies in bed and hears the bell,

and she shuts her eyes
and in her mind she sees that cowbell swing,
and she hugs that cow's wide neck,
and she feels that cow's pink nose,
so the girl owns the cow.

The cow gives the milk that she makes by eating grass,

10

and the farmer sells the milk to the dairy in the town,

and the milkman from the dairy drives his truck from house to house.

12

The owner of the dairy pays the milkman every day,

and the milkman buys some groceries

and goes home to cook a meal.

15

And the milkman and his family all sit down and eat,
and they wouldn't have their supper

if the cow did not make milk, so the milkman owns the cow.

The painter on vacation sees the cow and makes a sketch,

and she takes her sketch back home,
and she works for quite a stretch

till she's painted up a storm,
and the cow is in the painting,
so the painter owns the cow.

When the farmer cleans the barn each spring
there's lots of cow manure.
It's from the cow who ate the grass

22

that grows out in the field.
The farmer takes this fertilizer
and mixes it with straw,

and he spreads it on his garden
when the ground begins to thaw.

And when it's time to plant the seeds,
the soil is rich and black,

and the seeds grow into seedlings,
and the seedlings turn to plants,
and the plants put out their flowers
for the bees and dragonflies,

and the flowers turn to pumpkins
and to peas and beans and squash,
and the soil becomes a garden,
so the garden owns the cow.

A boy looks out the window
from the back seat of a car,
and he sees a foggy hillside
that is mostly gray and green.
Then he sees the cow so white,
and he sees the cow so black,

and the picture is so clear
that every foggy day
in every summer of his life,
he can see that foggy hillside
and that cow all black and white,
so the boy owns the cow.

And the boy who saw his foggy cow so many years ago,
sits down one night to write and write
and write about that cow.

And the words he wrote about his cow
are in this book that you read now.

So now who owns the cow?